Let's Rodeo!

Let's Rodeo!

Young Buckaroos and the World's Wildest Sport

ROBERT CRUM

Simon & Schuster Books for Young Readers

For Margie and Hannah

The author would like to express his appreciation to the Jenkinson family of Springfield, Oregon, and the Coleman family of Mollala, Oregon, for their enthusiastic help with this book. Much thanks also to the children, parents, and officials of the Northwest Peewee Rodeo Association.

SIMON & SCHUSTER BOOKS FOR YOUNG READERS
An imprint of Simon & Schuster Children's Publishing Division
1230 Avenue of the Americas
New York, New York 10020
Copyright © 1996 by Robert Crum
SIMON & SCHUSTER BOOKS FOR YOUNG READERS is a trademark of Simon & Schuster.
Book design by Susan M. Sherman
The text of this book is set in Baskerville, by Monotype.
Printed and bound in Singapore
First Edition
10 9 8 7 6 5 4 3 2 1

Library of Congress Cataloging-in-Publication Data

Crum, Robert.
    Let's Rodeo! : Young buckaroos and the world's wildest sport / by Robert Crum. — 1st ed.
        p.   cm.
    Includes bibliographical references and index.
1. Rodeos for children—Juvenile literature.   I. Title.
GV1834.4.C78   1996   791.8'4'083—dc20   95-43540
CIP   AC
ISBN 0-689-80075-4

Young cowboys and cowgirls have been doing rodeo for as long as grownups have—which means since around the mid-1800s, when buckaroos from different cattle drives challenged each other at what they did best. Just as kids do now, they learned by watching their parents and then trying it out themselves. And their parents encouraged them, knowing that a life spent working with animals requires the courage and skills that are most necessary in a rodeo. Indeed, some of the skills, like team roping, are the very ones that are still used on a ranch. Others, like barrel racing, teach important horse-handling skills.

Today there are a number of rodeo associations for kids to compete in, from national organizations such as the National Little Britches Rodeo Association, with around 5,800 members and more than 154 rodeos a year in 34 states, to regional groups like the Northwest Peewee Rodeo Association, with seven rodeos for its 400 members in western Oregon. Rodeos also take place in other parts of the country besides the West. The largest percentage of kids competing in Little Britches rodeos are actually from the southern state of Louisiana. There are also Little Britches rodeos in states quite distant from the West, like New Jersey, Tennessee, and Florida.

But rodeo is more than a sport; it's also a way of life that entails practice and responsibilities. It means learning how to care for your horse and equipment; it means spending time with your family on the weekends; and it means helping your friends, even though you may be each other's fiercest competitors.

Krystle Jenkinson bearing the flag during grand entry.

❋ Grand Entry

If it's summer and a Saturday and somewhere out West, someplace where the sky seems to go on forever over the rolling plains and high mountains, then it's quite likely that there are kids nearby who are finishing up their chores and putting on their best wrangling clothes, and heading with their folks into town. It's important not to be late, for today is the day of the junior rodeo. And the first event, grand entry, is one of the best events of all! This is when everyone mounts their horses and parades into the arena at a proud lope. It's when the announcer introduces the royalty—the rodeo queen and her court—as they gallop into the arena and wave. Then he introduces the girl who gets to sing the National Anthem. When she starts singing, everyone takes off their hats, and the rodeo queen gallops around the arena with the flag raised high and flapping in the wind. And then a cowboy prayer is recited, and a speech or two by some sponsors, wishing everyone a safe ride.

As though to drive the point home, there's the sound of a bareback bronc slamming its hooves against the sides of the bucking chutes. The horse knows it's going to be bucking in the arena soon and it's ready to have at it. Its hooves hit the chute with a sound like a cannon shot—enough to humble the cockiest cowboy.

Cowboys doff their hats for the flag.

✷Mutton Busting✷

This is how it begins, on the back of a surging animal, with the wind in your face, holding on for dear life. This is how most of the professional rodeo riders begin their careers, and the college champions, and the weekend amateurs—at four or five years old, with some thirty other children let loose from a pen on the backs of sheep. The sheep bolts from the pen surprisingly fast, enough to throw your head back as it takes off. You dig your hands into the wool and hold on as the sheep veers and darts. Like other rodeo animals, they're impossible to steer! If your sheep happens to make it to the other end of the arena first, and if you happen to hold on the whole way, you win a belt buckle. But even if you do a belly flop into the dust and your sheep goes sprinting away without you, you'll stand up, shaking with a thrill that goes deep.

That thrill is the love of rodeo. It's the same thrill felt by the first person who, long before recorded history, got the idea in his head to catch a wild horse and ride. For as long as they're on the animal, they become part of it. The animal's power and energy is theirs.

Rodeo champions of the future on their first ride.

Bareback

This is usually the first major event of the day—riding a powder keg of a horse without a saddle, one hand in the air. It sets the tone for the rest of the rodeo—one of excitement, quick action, strength, skill, and raw courage in the face of danger.

"Cowboy up!" the riders say to encourage each other. The phrase applies especially well in this event.

A rider comes out of the chute on a bareback bronc in a position that might make you think he were lying down for a nap. His feet are up around the horse's neck and his back is almost prone against the horse's back. But one look at his grimace tells a different story. Even before the gate is open, his jaw is clenched and his eyes are squinting half-closed. A nod is his signal to open the gate, yet his neck muscles are so tight he can barely manage that.

When the horse leaves the chute, the cowboy's spurs should be making contact just ahead of the horse's shoulders. The horse swings into the arena, almost slowly at first. Lying back and reaching forward with his spurs, the cowboy sees his friends standing on the chutes shift away. It's a short instant that seems to last forever as

the horse gathers its power. According to one cowboy, "That first second as you come out of the chute, you feel like you're being delivered to your fate on a platter."

And then your fate hits: an avalanche of bucks and kicks that would bury you in a second if you let it. The jolts yank at your arm and bang the knuckles of your gloved hand holding onto the rigging—the strap tied around the horse just behind the shoulders. Keeping that arm straight, a good rider maintains his backward tilt throughout the ride, keeping his seat firm against the horse, and pumping with his knees in rhythm with the horse. Without that backward lean, he would start bouncing off his seat on the horse, and a good pop from the horse would send him flying.

Twelve-year-old Krystle Jenkinson from Springfield, Oregon, says, "I felt like I had a real breakthrough at a rough stock clinic this last spring when, after finishing one bareback ride, I could actually remember each second of the ride—each buck and jump of the horse, and what my response was, what I did wrong and what I did right. Before that ride, everything was a jumble. I was just holding on. But after that ride, I felt I was more

Bareback: like riding a jackhammer as though it were a pogo stick.

in control. One thing they stressed in the clinic was the idea of 'minding the middle.' That means you have to center yourself on the horse and keep finding your balance during the ride."

As in all bucking events, older cowboys are required to stay on for eight seconds. For many younger riders, six seconds is all that's required, and they aren't disqualified if they don't ride with one hand or don't use their spurs—though they get more points if they do. At some rodeos, they are also required to wear hockey or football helmets instead of cowboy hats. Because the horse is still bucking after the ride is over, the rider often has to hold on until the pickup men can come by on horseback and lift him off.

And if the cowboy falls off before the eight seconds are up, he may walk out of the arena with the announcer's words ringing in his ears: "Let's give a big hand to that cowboy, folks, 'cause the only thing he's going home with tonight is your applause."

(left) Cort Huserik, 6, "catches air" during a bareback ride.

Krystle Jenkinson practicing on a bucking barrel.

Goat Tying

A young goat tier making the sport look easy.

It sounds easy enough. All you have to do is ride your horse out to the center of the arena where a young goat is tied at a stake, hop off your horse, and then tie a ribbon around the goat's tail. When you're done, you snap your arms into the air and the referee clicks the stopwatch. The best time wins.

But there are problems that arise along the way.

For instance, some of the goat tiers are only three years old. If they can't ride a horse, their mom or dad takes the horse by the bridle and guides them along. If they can, then chances are they can't get it to stop. Jumping off a moving horse is pretty hard, and many a goat tier lands face down in the dust. And then there's the problem of tying the ribbon. Some goat tiers haven't learned yet how to tie their own shoes, so tying a knot around a tail requires a lot of time and a lot of luck. It helps to hold the goat in place by straddling it or throwing an arm around it, though they still tend to slip away.

The tail is short. It wiggles as though attached by a spring. The announcer is making some joke about you, and laughter rises from the audience. The referee is giving you advice, telling you to straddle the goat, but as you lift your leg the goat darts away and you do a seat drop in the dirt. It's enough to make a goat tier cry. And sometimes, after five minutes, that's just what happens.

But by the end of the season—older, wiser, and practiced—you've gotten better. Your horse is still in stride as you leap off it at a pace that takes you directly to the rope, which you follow directly to the goat. You hold the goat in place with an arm as you tie the ribbon. And then you snap your arms in the air. All in one motion!

As you get older, more skills are required. The goats are bigger. You have to toss the goat on its side and tie three of its legs. And when you get even older you can move on to calf roping. But for now, goat tying is a world to itself, with as much triumph and heartbreak as any sport.

Lindsey Laubsch holding a "kid."

15

Breakaway Roping, Calf Roping, and Team Roping

Jennifer Jenkinson practices roping with a dummy.

The roping events test skills that are used every day on a ranch. When it's time to doctor or brand the cattle, or when it's time to move them from one pasture to another, roping skills are often called upon. These events may be more subtle than bronc or bull riding, but that does not mean they're any less difficult. In fact, while a bronc or bull rider has to concentrate on one thing—staying on—the roper has to concentrate on several things at the same time.

In breakaway roping, the calf is released from a chute, at which point the rider charges out after it (starting the judge's stopwatch), with a rope twirling in the air. The rope is attached by a light string to the saddle horn. The roper tosses the lasso around the calf's head and releases it. The watch is stopped when the steer reaches the end of the rope and pops the string off the saddle horn.

Calf roping, an event for older kids, is similar to breakaway, but it adds more challenges. This time the rope is tied directly to the saddle horn. When the loop falls around the calf's head, the roper quickly dismounts and follows the rope to the calf. The roper tosses the calf

Mitch Coleman uses his roping skills on his father's ranch.

A young calf roper homing in on her target.

The header ropes the head, and the heeler aims for the hind legs.

on its side and ties three of its legs with a "piggen string"—a short length of rope usually carried in the contestant's mouth. The clock is stopped when the roper's arms snap up in the air. However, if the calf wiggles free of the piggen string in the next six seconds, the ride is disqualified.

Team roping is even more complicated, since it requires coordination between two ropers—the "header" and the "heeler." Steers are also used, instead of calves. The header throws the rope around the steer's head, neck, or horns, and immediately takes a "dally"—

two turns of the rope around the saddle horn. (Without a dally, a roper trying to stop a 700-pound steer with only one hand would be asking for a huge rope burn.) The header then turns the steer into position for the heeler, who must catch both of the steer's hind legs.

Because the rider is usually busy throwing the rope, a smart, fast horse—one that can follow the steer or calf on its own—is essential. Such horses are usually as highly trained as the riders and are fascinating to watch as they torpedo after the calf, then automatically back up after the calf is roped in order to keep the rope taut.

Barrel Racing and Pole Bending

When Krystle Jenkinson enters the arena to compete in barrel racing, her first challenge is to keep her horse from bolting across the starting line. Yucca, a bay-colored quarter horse, has trained for this for hours and hours, and it wants to get going! Krystle tries to settle the horse by turning it away from the starting line, and when she gives the signal—a click of the tongue—the horse spins around, almost rearing, and gallops for the first barrel.

Barrel racing is performed in a cloverleaf pattern around three barrels. Two barrels are placed at opposite sides in the middle of the course; another is placed at the opposite end that the rider starts from. The rider circles each barrel once, making at least two of the turns around the barrels in opposite directions—a challenge to most horses, which, like people, tend to favor their right or left sides.

Krystle tells Yucca to whoa and reins in her gallop at the first barrel. The secret is to make the turn as tight as possible without knocking over the barrel—an accident that would add a five-second penalty to her score. She races to the next barrel, circles, then dashes for the last one. Circling the final barrel, Yucca explodes into a gallop, racing the last stretch back to where she started. An eighteen-second time is a decent time, and Krystle comes in just under.

"Yucca took that first barrel a little wide," she says, "and that cut down on my time. She had a strong final run, though."

Eleven-year-old Krystle Lovel from Canby, Oregon, says, "Barrel racing is highly competitive. The horses can cost more than $20,000, and in some barrel racing championships, a winner can make up to $40,000. You feel the intensity of it even in the peewee associations. You have to practice every day and be really focused. I find that it helps to run through a course in my head just before the actual run. And when you're running the course, you want to avoid any wasted motions. You want to cut as close to the barrel as you can without knocking it over. Though sometimes you do. I've got the bruises on my shins to prove it."

Krystle Jenkinson taking Yucca around a barrel.

Jennifer Jenkinson rounding a pole in pole bending.

Pole bending is often seen as preparation for barrel racing, though it is also good preparation for any sort of horse handling. The course is a series of six poles set about twenty feet apart. The rider runs the horse straight to the last pole, and then threads the horse back through them, as in a slalom course. An accomplished rider talks to the horse, telling it when to turn. Pulling one way and then the other with the reins, and urging the horse on with little kicks to the side, the rider and the horse become one smooth running animal.

If a horse goes off course so much that a decent time is impossible, the rider never gives up. That would send the wrong message to the horse. In order to help the horse learn the pattern, the rider must put the horse through its paces, even if it's in the middle of a championship competition.

The Competitors

"I rode in my first rough stock event today," says seven-year-old Lindsey Laubsch, who lives in Aurora, Oregon. "Bareback bronc on a Shetland pony! You should have seen what my dad made me wear. A hockey helmet with a face guard. A mouthpiece. A protective vest that went down to my knees. Leather chaps. A neck brace. Work boots with extra socks. We even stuffed some extra padding into the seat of my pants. When I got up on the chute to get on the horse, I saw my mom off to the side, biting her nails. I have to admit that I was a little scared, too. No, actually I was a lot scared. But I wanted to do it. And I sure did—the full six seconds. I even bailed off the horse by myself when the ride was over. The announcer told me to turn around and wave to the crowd, and I got a big cheer."

"We've got about four hundred head of cattle on our ranch, so roping is something I do every day," says Mitch Coleman, ten years old, from Mollala, Oregon. "Still, bareback is my favorite event. We've got a bucking machine in our hayshed that I practice on. You can set it for different speeds and even for different kinds of bucks. A lot of times my friends come over here to practice. My dad was a pro for nineteen years and he knows a lot of pros who are still competing, so when the big pro rodeo comes to town on July 4, some of them stay over at our place. Then my friends and I get to practice with them out in our corral."

"Calf ropers probably spend a lot more time roping practice dummies than they do roping calves," says eleven-year-old Tim Zacharias of Mulino, Oregon. He brings his dummy to the rodeos to practice with when he's not competing. "The secret of keeping the loop of the rope open is to turn your wrist and rotate your elbow. You throw right at the head, and then, when it wraps around the horns, you pull tight to take up the slack. You've got to do it without thinking, because when you're out there on a horse chasing a real calf, there's too much else to think about."

"I love the rodeo," says eleven-year-old Billy Bob Peterson, who lives in Junction City, Oregon. "My goal is to be a pro rodeo cowboy when I get older and someday compete in the National Finals Rodeo. I know it'll take a lot of work and practice getting there, 'cause I've seen what my dad goes through to compete in the pro rodeo circuit. But I'm willin'. Last year, I got my front teeth knocked out by a bull. I got popped off the bull and hit the ground, and when I raised my head, I got hooked in the mouth by its horns. So, yeah, I'm sometimes scared of those bulls. You'd have to be crazy not to be. But you really can't think about it too much, or else you'd never ride at all."

"In the rodeo association that I compete in, the Board of Directors elects the members of the rodeo royalty," says fourteen-year-old Tamara Henderson, of Silverton, Oregon, who is this year's reigning queen for the Northwest Peewee Rodeo Association. "It's a pretty big responsibility. I don't think there's a single weekend throughout the whole summer in which we aren't active in some rodeo. Sometimes we're just representing our association in parades. We also have to present the flag during the grand entry. For that we wear our fanciest cowgirl blouses—shiny satin with real nice embroidery. But after grand entry I have to rush back to the trailer and change into something else, because sometime in the next hour I'll be riding bulls."

Rodeo Clothing

Hats: Whether on a bucking horse or chasing down a calf, most rodeo riders lose their hats within the first few seconds of entering the arena. Nevertheless, riders are never without them. Western hats were created first by John Stetson—thus the term *Stetsons*. With their wide brims, they serve well in keeping sun and rain off the head.

Chaps: These leather leggings with wide flaps are worn by rodeo riders for protection while being thrown. They are often made by the rider, and are highly decorated.

Boots: Western boots are designed for several purposes. The high heel keeps the foot from slipping through the stirrup, and the loose top helps the boot slip off if it does get caught. The pointed toes help the rider slip into the stirrup. The stitching is not merely decorative; it also helps to strengthen the leather.

Gloves: Made of sturdy leather, they prevent rope burns and bruised knuckles.

Spurs: Strapped around the heel of a boot, they inspire fierce bucking from the animals. To prevent injury to the animals, rodeo regulations require that the rowels (the actual points) on the spurs be filed down.

Stock Contractor and Rough Stock

Most of the riders who compete in the gaming events—the events that require mastery and control of one's horse—ride their own horses at the rodeo. But the rough stock—the bucking horses and the bulls—is supplied by a stock contractor who specializes in such animals. Which cowboy rides which animal is determined by lottery before the rodeo begins.

"Everybody wants the toughest ride possible," says Joe Wiess, a stock contractor from Yoncalla, Oregon. "It might be a lot easier to ride an animal that doesn't buck or spin much, but you're not going to win any contests that way. Take Devil's Delight here," he says, pointing to a crossbred Brahma bull with a huge shoulder hump and horns a foot and a half long. "Devil's Delight weighs just under a ton, and you might think that with all that bulk he'd be a bit slow. Well, he can do eleven revolutions in eight seconds. He belly rolls while he's spinning, trying to throw the rider off the side, and the whole time he's surging from front to back like a tidal wave, and whipping those horns from side to side. Now that's a bull that a rider would be pleased to draw. That's what they call a 'money bull.'"

Joe and his employees keep busy at the rodeo, setting the animals up in the chutes, wrapping the horns that might need protection, and making sure they're fed, cared for, well rested, and in high spirits—ready for their eight seconds of hard work once or twice a week.

"It's not a bad life, to be a rodeo bull or a bronc," Joe says. "In fact, if it weren't for the rodeo, many of these animals would have been sent off for slaughter a long time ago. They're just too dangerous to have around a ranch. But now they've got it made. They eat well. They're clean. They don't work hard. They're taken from rodeo to rodeo in a large, safe semi-trailer. Stock contractors stake their reputations on providing healthy animals. If I let a bull that's limping into the arena, everybody's going to be down my throat for providing a bull that isn't going to win anybody any money."

Menu *for rodeo animals provided by the stock contractor (30 bulls, 25 calves, 30 steers, and 40 horses):*

>*2 1/2 tons of hay*
>*200 pounds of grain*
>*1500 gallons of water*

After a bull throws a rider, it turns around and comes looking.

☀Cowboy Up!☀

When you look toward the bucking chutes from the grandstands, one thing you're likely to see is a line of riders sitting on the fences. It's a scene that has been common ever since the days of the Old West, whether in rodeos or on a ranch where the workers are moving cattle from one fenced area to another. Western attire is a must for rodeo riders. In fact, rodeo associations rule that contestants must wear long-sleeved shirts (tucked in and with the sleeves rolled down), Western belts, Western boots, and Western hats.

Western wear is the standard at rodeos.

Cowboys have always been great "fence sitters."

Young riders learn a lot from watching how the pros do it.

"I think the greatest place to be during a rodeo is behind the chutes, when they're running broncs or bulls," says eleven-year-old Garrett Huserik from Mollala, Oregon. "It seems like everybody's pals with everybody else back there, even though they're competing against each other. The little kids all look up to the older kids, and the older kids are more than willing to help the little kids. And there's all this activity! The gates are all slamming as the animals charge into the chutes, and everybody's putting on their gloves and helmets, and then mounting up. And then everybody climbs up on the chutes to see the riders as their chutes open. It's funny, but you find yourself cheering even for the guys who score higher than you, because you feel like you've been part of it. It's one big team effort."

Rodeo is one of the few sports in which the fiercest competitors may also be the best of friends. There are several reasons for this. First, rodeo is a hard job that takes a lot of cooperation. Getting the rigging onto a bronc or a bull and then getting on that animal yourself is no easy task. The intense activity that goes on behind the chutes usually requires that you help the person that you'll soon be riding against. Another reason is that rodeo riders are strongly individualistic, which means that when they compete, the main person they are competing against is themselves. It's also the nature of many of the cowboys to be friendly and open. Many were raised on ranches and in small towns where people still don't lock their doors.

Practice begins early in rodeo.

Finally, there's the danger involved in the rodeo, which unites them as a group. Danger is always present at a rodeo. It's said that there are two kinds of rodeo riders: those who have been hurt and those who are going to be hurt. Indeed, anyone in the arena is at risk, including the judges, gate openers, and pickup men. It's common to see everyone in the arena running for the fences when an animal comes their way. Riders are at risk even inside the chutes, because a bronc can sometimes rear inside the chute and a one-ton bull can break a rider's leg merely by pressing with all its weight against the side of the chute. Out in the arena, most of the accidents occur not because of falling or getting gored, but by getting stomped. When jumping, a bronc or a bull slams its entire weight down on its rear feet, and if a fallen rider happens to be there, broken limbs or ribs are possible.

Fear is real among the riders, and the cowboy or cowgirl who said they never felt it would be lying. But rodeo riders have developed an attitude about fear that distinguishes them as a hardy breed. Fear, they say, gets in the way of your concentration. If you're scared, the chances that you might get thrown by the bronc or bull increase, along with the chances that you might get hurt. Best to put the fear out of your mind and concentrate on what you have to do.

Which is what a rider means by the phrase, "Cowboy up!"

Saddle Bronc

Behind the chutes, a call goes up: "Heads up! Broncs coming through!" With feet pounding and manes flying, the saddle broncs enter the chutes from the holding pens. As each one reaches the spot where it can be saddled and mounted, wooden barriers boom shut one after another.

A saddle on a bucking horse might seem to make it an easier event than riding bareback broncs. But consider this: if your horse throws you and one of your feet gets caught in the stirrup, you could be dragged from one end of the arena to the other before the pickup men and judges manage to get you free. The horse is still bucking and those four hooves are slamming around your head. For this reason, many saddle bronc riders wear boots a size too big. If they get stuck in the stirrup, it's easier to slip out. The risk involved in saddle bronc is also why many rodeo associations require that the competitors wait until they're in high school before they can do it.

Back at the chutes, the cowboys are setting their grip on the rein (too high a grip may cause a rider to be thrown over the rear of the horse; too low to be thrown over the front). The cowboys make sure the saddle is on tight. The flank strap is readied around the horse's flank. All in all, the careful preparations seem like those for an astronaut being readied for launch.

And in a way, the cowboy will indeed be launched. As in bareback bronc, the rider must leave the chute with the spurs making contact ahead of the horse's shoulders, and one hand must be kept in the air at all times. The horse may be a "runaway bucker," racing wildly halfway across the arena before it explodes in a cascade of bucks, or it may be a "spinner," turning and bucking in tight circles. Some horses "sunfish" in the middle of their bucks, rolling their bellies sideways and up, and some may "suck in their backs" toward their stomachs as they leap, which makes the cowboy feel as though he's dropping down an elevator shaft. Whatever the horse's style, the name that the cowboy gives to the back of a bronc or a bull is fitting: they call it the "hurricane deck." The cowboys also have a phrase for the first six seconds of the ride, the fiercest part, during which the horse may jump as many as twenty times. They call it "riding out the storm."

Saddle bronc isn't just a matter of holding on;
it's holding on with style.

The clown's job is to distract the bull.

Clowns

Rodeo clowns always seem to be doing one thing or another outrageously wrong, much to the amusement of the crowd. They'll pretend to be nearsighted and shake hands with the tail of a bull.

Or they'll taunt a bull into chasing them, then dive headfirst into a foam-padded barrel. When the bull slams into the barrel with all its might, the clown waves a white flag of surrender.

With their shenanigans, their baggy clothes, and their painted faces, the rodeo clowns are a funny sight indeed. But their costumes serve a very serious purpose. To know why bull riders have so much respect for the clowns (very few would even get on the bull if there weren't a clown in the arena), imagine yourself in this situation: You've just held on to the back of a raging, spinning, bucking, 2,000-pound bull for eight seconds (or probably less), tossed every which way until you barely know up from down, and finally you're tossed off like a rag doll. You land belly down in the muddy arena (rodeos are held rain or shine), with the wind knocked out of you. You try to get up but can't: the mud is too heavy and keeps sucking you back. And the bull, in a flash, turns around to confront whatever was on his back that was making him so mad: namely, you.

This is where the rodeo clowns—also called bullfighters—earn their respect. Pickup men are useless during bull riding. Because their horses would be gored by the bull, their job in this event is to escort (at a distance) the bull to the exit gate. But this can be done only after the bull has been distracted from the cowboy lying in the dirt. That's where the painted face and baggy clothes of the clown come in handy. They offer the bull an aggravating distraction. The clown, in other words, offers himself as bait to the bull.

His only protection is his quickness and agility, and occasionally a foam barrel to jump into, but only after the rider is safe, and only if he can reach it in time. The baggy clothes are also a help; they rip easily when hooked by the bull's horns. Bullfighting also takes stamina, since a clown may face as many as eighteen bulls at a single rodeo, while a cowboy rides no more than one.

In essence, the rodeo clown's business is to save lives while playing the fool.

Bull Riding

Back behind the chutes, the bull riders are getting their riding gloves rosined up by pulling hard on a rosin-covered rope. The sticky rosin helps them keep their grip. To keep the glove itself from slipping off, they wind a strap of leather around the wrist of the glove and tie it tight. Then it's time to climb up on the chutes and lower themselves onto the bulls.

The bulls have names like TNT, Bam-bam, T. Rex, Turbo, Thunderation, Heavy Metal, Stomper, Torpedo, Knockout, Dynamo. . . .

A young bull rider "rosining up."

When you see the bulls out in the arena, they seem like cold-blooded engines of destruction. So when it comes time to sit down on one in the chutes (first stepping lightly on its back so that it knows you're coming), you're always a little surprised to feel that the bull is radiating warmth. But you don't think about it too long, because it also radiates sheer power. When it turns its head, the horns graze your thigh. And though you feel that the horns are massive, heavy, and solid as rock, you know the bull can whip them around as though they were made of Styrofoam.

Peewee and junior kids ride bulls that are smaller, but pound for pound they can be just as fierce. In some rodeo associations, helmets, mouthpieces, and protective vests are required for kids.

"My hands are always shaking when I get up on a bull," says Krystle Jenkinson. "But it helps me to

remember all the times I saw older, professional bull riders get up on their bulls with shaking hands."

"When I'm sitting up there on that bull in the chute," says Mitch Coleman, "I'm mostly trying to remember what I know about the bull. I've looked at him off and on throughout the day, and I've talked to other people who have ridden him in the past. So I know if he tends to start spinning as he leaves the chute or if he'll blow out of there. Still, it's hard to remember that stuff, 'cause you're so jittery up there."

The rigging goes around the bull just behind the bull's shoulder hump. It has a slot like the handle of a duffel bag that your gloved hand slips into. From the bottom of the rigging—behind the bull's front legs—hangs a cowbell, which is meant to irritate the bull into jumping harder. You fasten your hand to the rigging with several wraps of rope.

Then comes the moment when you have to give the nod for the gate to open. The rules require that older kids and pros have to touch their spurs to the bull as it leaves the chute. They also have to ride with one hand in the air.

Bulls move with startling speed. Though they might weigh more than a ton (the average weight is 1,500 pounds—as much as a small car), they can jump more than three feet in the air. Bulls respond with more pitches and sideway rolls than broncs. A bull's skin is also looser than a bronc's, making it harder to stay on.

Riders and animals alike—both are athletes.

A bull explodes from the chutes.

But the chief difference—and this is how the bull riders really earn their buckles—is that bulls spin.

Some bulls spin so fast that they're like merry-go-rounds gone crazy. They create their own centrifugal force, pushing you off-center and away from the bull. The only way to counteract the centrifugal force is to do what common sense tells you not to do: lean partway into the spin and look down into what bull riders call "the well." The bull, however, can change the direction of its spinning in a flash, and if you don't react as quickly, leaning at the correct angle into the new well on the other side, you'll be thrown.

"My favorite event is bulls," says John Morehouse, a thirteen-year-old bull rider from Christmas Valley, Oregon. "In fact, it's all I do. My dad says that when he was a pro, bulls were his favorite, too, because they only broke his bones once, while the broncs broke his bones

When you hit the dirt, you better hit it running.

thirty-one times. A lot of people think that bull riding is just a matter of strength and holding on. But you have to think fast out there, and you have to be coordinated."

There's no shame in being thrown from a bull that might weigh fifteen to twenty times more than you. It happens to champions and beginners alike. But if you manage to stay on the full eight seconds, you'll hit the ground a changed person—one who has known, withstood, and even mastered the fury of the beast. You have countered its orneriest gyrations with subtle shifts of your weight. You have mastered its quick muscles with quick thinking. With one hand high in the air, you have straddled the earthquake, ridden the whirlwind, surfed the tidal wave.

The Buckles

After a rodeo season full of heat and dust, spills and bruises, a trophy buckle seems like the shiniest thing in the world. And well it should: it's made of sterling silver. Some are rectangular, some are oval, and they're all as big as a man's hand. They're engraved with a scroll and leaf pattern, or a lariat, and they usually carry a design representing the event for which they are awarded. Many are also engraved with the winner's name. Handmade, the buckles cost more than forty dollars.

No one knows how the tradition of honoring rodeo excellence with a belt buckle was started, but it has been around at least since the 1920s. In a way, they are the perfect award for a sport that combines everyday, practical skills with larger-than-life bravado. With the same combination of practicality and pride, the kids wear them at home and in school. They will be treasured for life. Every ounce of those shiny buckles has been earned with hard practice, bruises, and skill.

Buckles are the trophies of rodeo.

☀ Cowboy Prayer ☀

*O*ur Father and our God,
  who art the giver of all good life,
we pause at this time to give Thee thanks
for the many blessings that we enjoy at Thy bounty.
We pray, Oh Lord, that you bless each and
   every contestant,
not asking to draw around a chute fighting horse
or a steer that won't lay,
but that you would endow each of us
to do the best with the talent
with which Thou has blessed us,
so that when we make that last ride
up there where the grass is stirrup high
and the water runs cool, clear, and deep,
that you would tell us on our final ride
that our entry fees are paid.

Glossary

Association saddle: standard saddle used in saddle bronc events

Bail out: to voluntarily jump off a bronc or bull, as opposed to being thrown off

Bronc: a spirited horse used in bucking events. Also "bronco." From the Spanish *bronco,* meaning "wild."

Bucking chute: stalls where broncs and bulls are mounted by rodeo cowboys

Bullfighter: clown who distracts the bull in order to save the cowboy who has just come off it

Flank strap: a strap placed around a horse's belly and pulled tight in order to make it buck. Also called a "bucking strap."

Gaming events: events in which the winner completes a given task in the fastest time, as in the roping events, barrel racing, pole bending, and goat tying

Header: the person in team roping who ropes the steer's head

Heeler: the person in team roping who ropes the steer's hind legs

Hung up: to get caught in the rigging of a bareback bronc or a bull, or in the stirrups of a saddle bronc

Marking the horse: to leave the bucking chutes with your spurs just ahead of the horse's shoulders, as required by professional rodeo associations

Pickup men: two men at every rodeo who help bronco riders dismount from their horses after their eight-second ride is over

Piggen string: a short piece of rope used by a calf roper to tie the feet of the calf

Reride: another chance to ride given to a rough stock rider whose animal has not bucked well

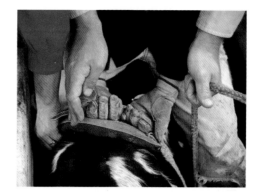

Rigging: the equipment used on a bull or bareback horse

Rough stock: horses and bulls provided by the stock contractor for bucking events

Index